PUBLISHED BY COLOUR LIBRARY BOOKS LTD
GODALMING, SURREY, ENGLAND
© 1988 PETER HADDOCK LTD
BRIDLINGTON, ENGLAND
Printed in Italy
ISBN 0 7105 0462 4

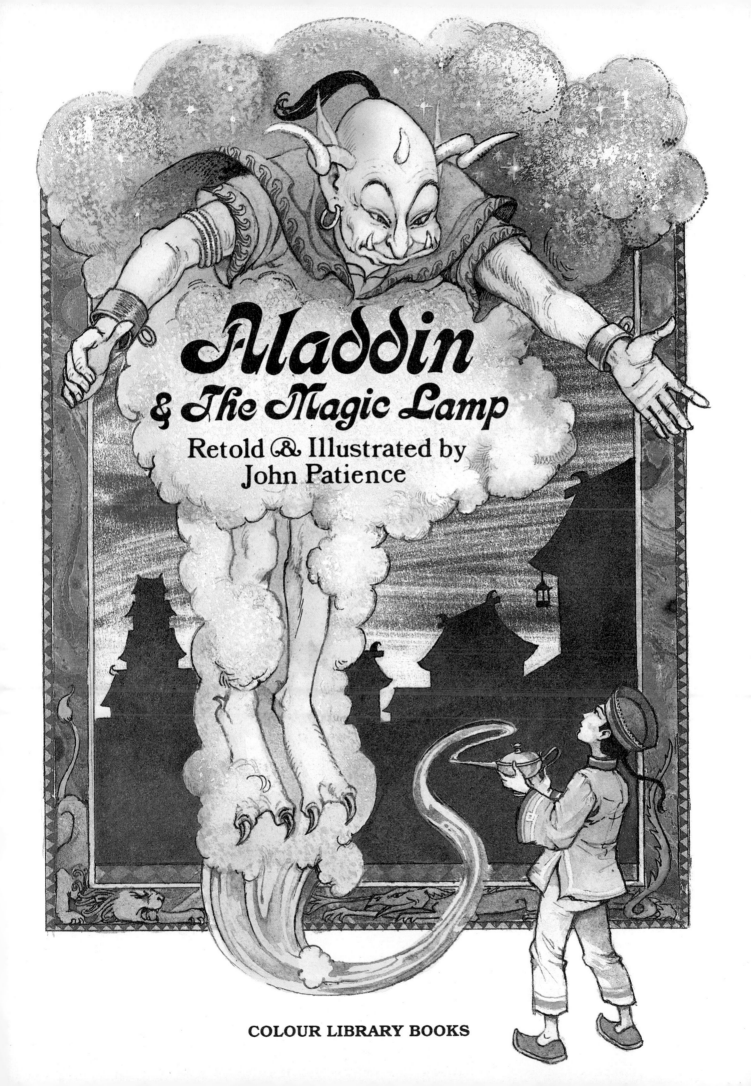

Aladdin
& The Magic Lamp

Retold & Illustrated by John Patience

COLOUR LIBRARY BOOKS

This is the story of a young man named Aladdin who lived with his widowed mother in a city in China, long, long ago. One day Aladdin was talking with his friends in the street when a stranger approached him. He was an evil magician called Abenazer who had travelled all the way from Africa to carry out a secret plan. "My boy," said Abenazer, "I can make you extremely rich if you will only help me with a small task." Now Aladdin and his mother were very poor and so he was eager and willing to help.

Abenazer took Aladdin to a place where a narrow tunnel led down into the mountainside. "At the end of the tunnel you will find a magic garden where precious jewels grow on trees," said the magician. "You may help yourself to them. All I want is the ancient bronze lamp that burns in the garden. There are dangers in the tunnel, but wear this ring and it will protect you."

Aladdin made his way down the tunnel to the magic garden where, as Abenazer had promised, he found the ancient lamp and the beautiful jewelled

trees. Snuffing out the lamp he put it into his pocket. He picked some of the jewels and then crept back up to the mouth of the tunnel. "I see you have the lamp!" cried Abenazer. "Give it to me at once!" Aladdin refused to do this until he was out of the tunnel. At this, Abenazer became extremely angry and, screaming out some magic words, he sealed up the tunnel's entrance, leaving Aladdin imprisoned underground.

For two days the boy remained, crying in the dark. Then he accidentally rubbed the ring which Abanezer had given him. Immediately an enormous genie appeared, saying, "I am the slave of the ring and am ready to obey you. What is your wish?" "Please take me out of this place," cried the startled Aladdin. In a moment he found himself standing outside the tunnel in the open air.

When Aladdin arrived back home, his mother was overjoyed to see him. He told her the story of his adventures and showed her the old brass lamp. "How strange," she said. "Why should Abenazer want this old lamp so badly? Look how dirty it is." And she rubbed it with her sleeve to shine it up. Suddenly there was a deafening BANG and a huge genie came pouring like smoke from the lamp, saying, "Behold, I am the genie of the lamp – the greatest of all the genies. What is your wish?" Aladdin's mother was terrified, but Aladdin, who had seen a genie before, replied, "I am hungry. Please fetch me something to eat." In a moment the kitchen table was spread with a marvellous feast. Aladdin quickly realised the incredible power of the lamp and why Abenazer had wanted it so much. He commanded the genie to bring fine clothes for his mother and himself and to transform their humble house into a grand palace, and in an instant it was done.

One day Aladdin happened to see the Emperor's daughter, the beautiful princess Badoobadoor riding by on her elephant, and he immediately fell in love with her. He decided there and then that he would marry her. Summoning the genie of the lamp, Aladdin gave his orders and the genie provided him with a dozen slaves, each with a basin filled with gold and jewels. Aladdin then went to visit the Emperor. Offering him the jewels, Aladdin proclaimed his love for princess Badoobadoor and begged for her hand in marriage. The Emperor was very impressed with Aladdin and his splendid gifts. As for Badoobadoor, she had fallen as deeply in love with Aladdin as he had with her. The Emperor gave his consent and they were married the next day.

However, the evil magician Abenazer had not forgotten Aladdin and the lamp and used his magic arts to discover that, instead of perishing in the cave, he had escaped and married the princess. Choosing a day when Aladdin was away on a hunting trip, Abenazer bought a dozen copper lamps, put them in a basket and disguised himself as a peddlar. He then went to the palace, crying, "New lamps for old. Bring me your old lamps and I will give you new ones for them!" The princess heard this strange cry and, remembering a dirty old lamp belonging to Aladdin, she sent a slave to fetch it and exchange if for a bright new one. Little did she know that she had given away Aladdin's most treasured possession.

Abenazer was filled with a wicked glee. The magic lamp was his at last! He went out of the city gates to a lonely place where he remained until nightfall, when he rubbed the lamp. The genie appeared and at Abenazer's command transported Aladdin's palace and the princess in it to a far-off place in Africa.

When Aladdin returned home he was amazed. Where was his palace, his beautiful wife and his magic lamp? Gone! What was he to do? He wrung his hands in despair and accidentally rubbed the magic ring. "What do you wish?" said the genie of the ring as he appeared. "Bring me back my palace and my dear wife," replied Aladdin. "What you ask," said the genie, "Is not within my power. Only the genie of the lamp can do that." "Then take me to the spot where my palace is," commanded

Aladdin. He had barely finished speaking before he heard the wind roaring in his ears as the genie picked him up and whisked him at incredible speed to Africa where the palace now stood. He set him down under a tree by Badoobadoor's window and disappeared. It was night and Aladdin slept soundly until next morning, when he was roused by the princess opening her window.

The princess was overjoyed to see Aladdin again and told him of how Abenazer held her prisoner and came to visit her every day. Aladdin gave her a deadly poison which he told her to pour into the magician's wine glass. Then he hid himself behind a screen. When Abenazer came to visit that day, instead of greeting him with tears and pleading for him to let her go, the princess welcomed him with a glass of poisoned wine. The magician accepted it eagerly, drained it to the last drop and fell down dead. Then Aladdin came out from his hiding place and, taking the lamp from Abenazer's pocket, he summoned the genie. "Take us home," he cried and in the winking of an eye the palace was back in China where it belonged. You may be sure that Aladdin and Badoobadoor lived there happily for the rest of their lives.